Lauren Flanagan

Reputation

Bumblebee Books
London

A CIP catalogue record for this title is
available from the British Library.

ISBN: 978-1-83934-249-3

Bumblebee Books is an imprint of
Olympia Publishers.

First Published in 2021

Bumblebee Books
Tallis House
2 Tallis Street
London
EC4Y 0AB

Printed in Great Britain

www.olympiapublishers.com

Dedication

To all the individuals who are more than their reputation.

You see in my classroom, I am known as the bad lad,
I always make my teacher, friends
or classmates frustrated and sad.

My behaviour, well it often drives everyone around me mad and my mum, well, she sees me as an annoyingly bad lad.

As for school I cannot take away and I can't quite add.

But ask me and I can show you how to use my bro's iPad.
Yeah it may not be right, but that's just too bad!
I'd like to practice but I have no
squared paper or writing pad.

Love, comfort and security, is something
I've never really had.

I have two older brothers, I think ones called Chad
But I never get to see them, like I don't see my dad.

When people see me, their faces
are no longer elated or glad,
You see I have a reputation at home and school,
I'm known as the troubled child or the bad lad.

But deep down, do you know what I really wish I had
Is lots of laughter and family around, as well as a goofy grandad.

So that one day, I will no longer be
that reputation of a bad lad,
The one who's looked or shouted at,
all day every day, not just a tad!

I have dreams too, my goal is to try my best in school and learn how to count and add.

So that one day I can stand tall and proud,
knowing I'm a university grad.

I don't want to keep making everyone around me angry, stressed or sad.

I try to stop my behaviour, driving my teacher crazy and other people mad.

When people see me, I want them
to be excited, proud and glad.
So please before you discriminate,
exclude or hold a grudge,
remember I don't want to continue
being bad, or to be misjudged.

I've had enough...

I no longer want the…

Reputation of being 'A BAD LAD'.

ANNOYING
WEIRDO
I'M NOT YOUR FRIEND
BAD LAD
STUPID
DON'T LIKE YOU
NAUGHTY
FREAK
UGLY
RUDE

About the Author

Lauren Flanagan was born in Camden, premature but with a will to survive. Having grown up in southeast London till now, Lauren knew from a young age her passion was to support children and went on to complete a Ba in education as well as a masters in inclusive special education. Lauren's second passion has been a love of reading and creative writing particularly poetry and writing texts that provokes thoughtful thinking and encourages positive change.

Acknowledgements

A huge thank you to the publishing and illustrating team. To Js'ade Stephenson, Emma Ramsden, Errol Flanagan, Stefan Flanagan and Clyde and Jo Berry, I am eternally grateful for everything!

Printed in Great Britain
by Amazon

83046783R00022